A Treasury of Classic
Fairy Tales

THE LAND OF STORIES

A TREASURY OF CLASSIC FAIRY TALES

CHRIS COLFER

ILLUSTRATED BY BRANDON DORMAN

L B

Little, Brown and Company
New York Boston

Copyright © 2016 by Christopher Colfer

Jacket and interior art copyright © 2016 by Brandon Dorman

Damask pattern art © emo_O/Shutterstock.com

Interior design by Sasha Illingworth

Little, Brown and Company

Hachette Book Group

1290 Avenue of the Americas, New York, NY 10104

Visit us at lb-kids.com

Little, Brown and Company is a division of Hachette Book Group, Inc.

The Little, Brown name and logo are trademarks of Hachette Book Group, Inc.

The publisher is not responsible for websites (or their content) that are not owned by the publisher.

First Edition: October 2016

ISBN 978-0-316-35591-9

10 9 8 7 6 5 4 3 2 1

WOR

Printed in the United States of America

To my mom.

Thank you for introducing me to fairy tales

and humoring my endless curiosity

about the characters and their motives.

I love you and will miss you always.

CONTENTS

Once upon a time, there were a brother and sister named Hansel and Gretel. They lived with their father and step-mother in a small cottage at the edge of the woods. Their father was a good man who loved his children more than anything else in the world. His wife, however, was a mean and selfish woman who became jealous of the affection her husband showed his children.

Their father was a woodcutter and did all he could to provide for his family, but due to a recent famine spreading across the land, times were hard for peasant families in the kingdom. Food was scarce, and many worried about surviving the approaching winter.

"If we don't do something, we'll starve!" the wife told the woodcutter one night before bed. "We barely have enough food for the two of us. We must get rid of Hansel and Gretel if we want to survive."

"I could never get rid of my children," the woodcutter said. "They mean everything to me!"

"It'll be easy," said the wife, who had already devised a plan. "Tomorrow, we'll take Hansel and Gretel deep into the forest and leave them there. They're so young, they won't be able to find their way home. They'll get lost and a hungry pack of wolves will find them. We'll never have to worry about feeding them again."

"I would rather starve than abandon my children," the woodcutter said. "I won't hear another word of this. We will find another way to get through the winter."

Despite her husband's wishes, the wife was convinced her plan was the only solution. Luckily, Hansel and Gretel were still awake and heard their father and stepmother's conversation through the thin walls of their cottage.

"What will we do, Hansel?" Gretel asked her brother. "Our stepmother will surely try to abandon us in the woods while Father is away chopping wood tomorrow."

"Don't fret, Gretel," Hansel said. "I'll gather white pebbles tonight while they sleep and create a trail to follow back home."

So Hansel snuck outside while his father and stepmother slept and gathered as many white pebbles as he could find. The next morning, once the woodcutter left to chop down trees, his wife led the children into the woods.

"Where are we going?" Gretel asked.

"To collect firewood," their stepmother said. "Now be quiet and follow me."

She led them deep into the heart of the forest, farther than Hansel and Gretel had ever gone before. Hansel dropped a white pebble every few steps, leaving a trail behind them. They traveled the whole day and came to a stop just as the sun began to set.

"Now look around and help me gather wood," their stepmother said. But before she finished her sentence, she dashed back in the direction from which they had come, leaving her stepchildren all alone in the woods.

Hansel and Gretel followed the trail of white pebbles to their cottage. The forest became so dark after nightfall, the small white stones were the only thing they could see. By the time they returned, their father was worried sick about them.

"Thank the Lord you're all right," the woodcutter said and embraced his children tightly. "Where is your stepmother?"

To Hansel and Gretel's surprise, they had arrived home before their stepmother. Without a trail of pebbles, the woodcutter's wife had a hard time navigating through the woods and returned several hours after her stepchildren. She was furious to see that Hansel and Gretel had found their way back to the cottage.

"What happened?" the woodcutter asked his wife.

"We went to retrieve firewood," the wife said. "I turned my back for one minute and they were gone."

"I pray it doesn't happen again," the woodcutter said.

"Don't worry, *it won't*," the wife said and glared at her stepchildren when her husband wasn't looking.

That night, the wife locked Hansel and Gretel in their room so they couldn't sneak out to collect any more white pebbles.

"Oh, Hansel, what are we to do now?" Gretel asked her brother. "Our stepmother will surely try to abandon us again tomorrow."

"Don't fret, Gretel," Hansel said. "Tomorrow morning at breakfast,

we'll save our crusts of bread and use bread crumbs to make a trail."

Just as predicted, as soon as their father left the next morning, their stepmother led Hansel and Gretel back into the woods. They walked even longer this time, traveling farther into the trees than ever before. Hansel left crumbs behind them as they went and nearly ran out by the time they stopped.

"Now gather up some wood," their stepmother said.

Once again, she dashed back toward the cottage and left Hansel and Gretel all alone in the woods. It was so late that Hansel and Gretel decided to sleep in the woods and wait for morning to follow the bread crumbs home. Unfortunately, by the time they awoke, the morning birds had eaten all the bread crumbs they'd left behind!

Hansel and Gretel walked through the woods in what they hoped was the right direction, but there were so many trees, it was impossible to tell. They walked for hours and hours, never finding a familiar part of the forest.

They finally found a friendly white bird and followed it through the woods, hoping it might lead them home. The longer they followed the bird, the more a wonderful aroma filled the air. It was a sweet smell, as if something delicious was baking in an oven nearby.

Hansel and Gretel came upon a clearing in the middle of the woods. They were delighted to see, in the center of the clearing, a house made

entirely of food. It had gingerbread walls, a fence made of candy canes, and a garden of gumdrop shrubs. The roof was covered in frosting, and the windows were made of clear sugar panes.

"I've never seen something so delicious!" Gretel exclaimed.

She and her brother dashed toward the house and began eating it. They were so hungry and tired from their journey, they didn't even think to ask the resident for permission. Suddenly, the door of the home opened and a kind-looking old woman stepped outside.

"Who's there?" the old woman said. "What are you doing to my house?"

"Please forgive us," Hansel said. "We were hungry and lost in the woods when we found your home."

The old woman smiled at them, showing rotting teeth behind her wrinkled lips.

"I didn't realize you were *children*," she said happily. "No need to apologize, my dear. I built a home out of food for children just like you. Please eat as much as you'd like!"

Hansel and Gretel were certain the old woman must be an angel in disguise. They ate the candy-cane fence and the gumdrop shrubs. They ate the sugar-pane windows and licked all the frosting off the roof. By the time Hansel and Gretel were full, they'd eaten everything but the gingerbread walls.

"Now come inside and rest, my dears," the old woman said. "There are more goodies and soft beds waiting for you."

Hansel and Gretel eagerly did as the old woman requested, knowing they could use a rest after their journey through the woods. However, when they went inside, there were no goodies or beds to be found, only a large cage and an enormous oven.

The old woman threw Hansel and Gretel in the cage and locked the door. She took off the mask of an old woman, and the children saw that the rest of her was as rotten as her teeth. She wasn't a sweet old woman at all, but *an ugly old witch*!

"One of you shall be my dinner, and the other shall be my slave!" the witch cackled. "That'll teach you not to wander the woods alone!"

The witch pulled Gretel out of the cage and handed her a broom.

"Sweep the house, girl," the witch ordered. "I want a clean home before my meal."

Not having much choice, Gretel swept the house until it was spotless. The witch lit a fire in the oven and then pulled Hansel out of the cage.

"You shouldn't eat me yet!" Hansel pleaded. "I'm too thin and frail to make a meal, but if you keep feeding me, soon I'll make a feast!"

The witch scratched the hairs on her chin and thought it over.

"That's an excellent idea," the witch said. "I shall keep feeding you until you outgrow the cage; then you shall be my first meal of winter!"

For weeks and weeks, the witch forced Hansel to eat delicious sweets, while Gretel was forced to clean inside and outside the house. At the end of every day, the witch would peer into the cage and squint at Hansel.

"Are you pleasantly plump yet?" the witch asked.

Hansel assumed the witch must have bad vision. Otherwise, surely she could see that his clothes were much tighter than before and he grew rounder every day. He quickly thought of a way to use the witch's failing eyes to save his life.

"I'd make a decent bite, but not enough to serve your appetite," Hansel lied.

The witch huffed and puffed, then ordered Gretel to cook her a rat stew for dinner.

The next day, as Gretel was cleaning up leaves outside the house, she put a couple of sticks in her pocket. Later that night, she slid them into Hansel's cage just before the witch peered inside.

"Are you reasonably round yet?" the witch asked.

"He's as thin as he's ever been," Gretel said. "Hansel, hold out your hand so the witch can feel your bony finger."

Gretel nodded to the sticks she had given him, and Hansel knew what to do. He held out one stick like it was a part of his hand, and the witch felt it. She moaned and groaned, then ordered Gretel to prepare spider soup for her supper.

Hansel and Gretel didn't know how much longer they could continue tricking the witch. They knew she was growing impatient, because the next day she peered into the cage even before the sun had set.

"Are you finally fat?" she asked.

"I'm ample for snacking, but a full meal you'd be lacking," Hansel lied again.

He held out a stick as he had done the night before. The witch felt the stick, and her face went bright red.

"I've waited long enough!" the witch shouted. "Fat or not, I will eat you tonight! Prepare the oven, girl!"

Gretel opened the wide door to the oven and filled it with firewood. She lit a match, and a healthy fire grew inside. The witch stood behind her, and a sinister smile grew across her ugly face.

"Now I want you to test the fire to see if it's hot," the witch said.

Gretel knew the witch was trying to trick her—she was going to eat both of them for dinner!

"But I don't know how," Gretel said, thinking fast. "Will you show me what to do?"

"Stupid girl," the witch said. "Move aside and I will show you. It's very simple; you just lean into the oven like this and touch the flames with your— *AAAAHHH!*"

Gretel pushed the witch into the oven with all her might and locked

the door behind her. The witch screamed as she was cooked to a crisp. When her screams finally came to a stop, Gretel freed Hansel from the cage. Just before they escaped the house, Hansel found a vase full of rubies and diamonds the witch had kept on a shelf. He and Gretel filled their pockets with the jewels and ran into the woods.

They ran far away from the witch's gingerbread house and never looked back. Eventually, they came to the edge of the woods and saw a very familiar cottage.

"Gretel, look! We're home!" Hansel exclaimed.

The woodcutter heard his children and rushed out to greet them. He was so overjoyed to see them that tears filled his eyes and rolled down his face. Hansel and Gretel looked around the cottage, but the woodcutter's wife was nowhere to be found.

"Father, what happened to our stepmother?" Gretel asked.

"The same day you went missing, she got lost in the woods and a pack of wolves found her," he said. "I was so worried the same had happened to you, but you're both alive and well, so all is right in the world!"

The woodcutter embraced his children and never let them out of his sight again. They used the jewels to buy a new home much closer to the nearby village, and Hansel and Gretel ate all the sweets they wanted without the fear of witches. The family survived the winter and lived happily ever after.

The End

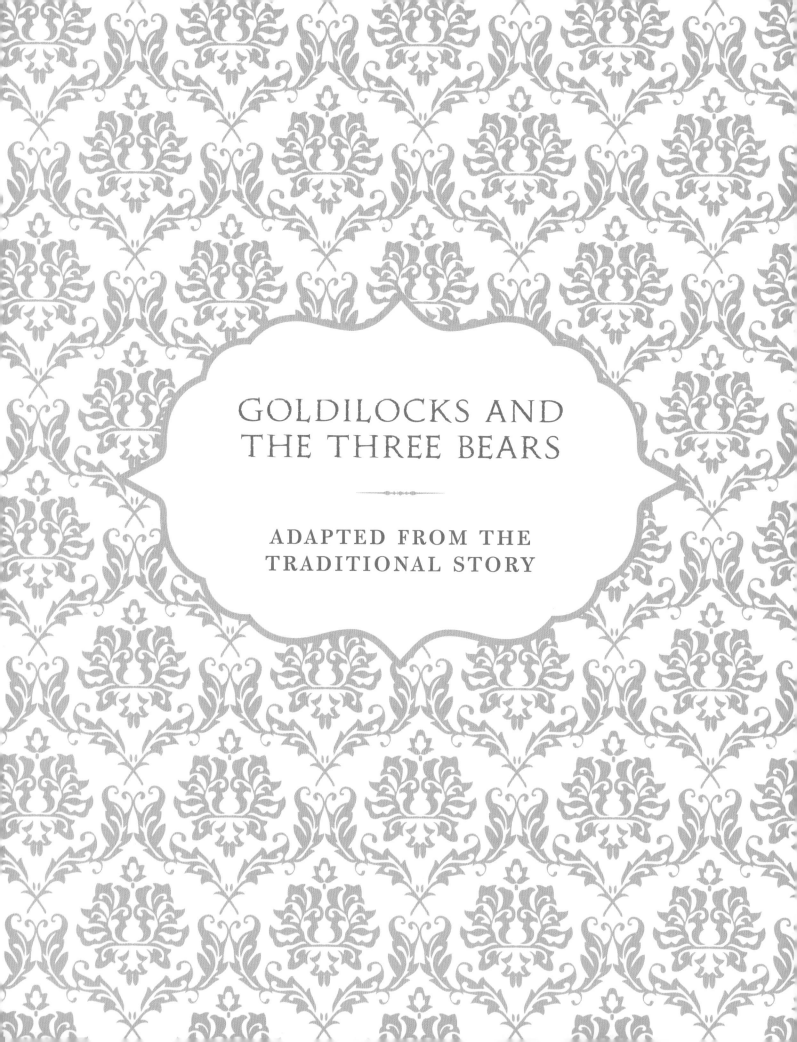

GOLDILOCKS AND THE THREE BEARS

ADAPTED FROM THE TRADITIONAL STORY

Jack leaped off the table with the harp in his arms, and they landed directly on the giant's foot.

"AAAAHHHH!" the giant yelled. He held his aching toes and hopped around the castle on one foot.

Jack held the harp in one arm and grabbed the bag of coins with the other. He ran to the door as fast as his legs would carry him. He crawled under the door and dashed down the paved road to the beanstalk.

Right when Jack made it back to the beanstalk, the giant emerged from the castle and ran down the path after him. Jack hurried down the beanstalk, but the giant followed, causing the beanstalk to sway among the clouds.

On the ground below, Jack's mother heard the commotion and ran out of the cottage to see what was happening. She was so frightened to see the giant chasing her son that it took her a couple of moments to find her voice.

"Jack! What have you gotten yourself into?" she yelled up at her son.

"Mother, get me the axe! I need to chop the beanstalk down before the giant reaches the ground!" Jack said.

The widow ran inside the house and returned with the axe. Jack reached the ground and took the axe from his mother. In one enormous swing, Jack chopped the beanstalk in two. It teetered over and the giant went with it, falling to his death.

"Jack, do you have any idea how worried I was about you?" the widow yelled.

"I'm sorry I made you worry, Mother," Jack said. "But I promise you'll never have to worry about anything ever again. Look what I've brought home!"

Jack emptied the bag of gold coins he'd collected at the giant's castle and showed them to his mother. The widow was so overjoyed, tears

came to her eyes. She hugged her son tightly and kissed his cheek.

"My brave boy!" she said. "You've saved us! We'll never go hungry again!"

Jack and the widow used the coins to build a new home and started a proper farm that grew more crops than they knew what to do with. They ate three meals a day, and the harp sang them beautiful songs every night before bed.

The old man's promise turned out to be true: The magic beans gave Jack all of his heart's greatest desires. But the true magic was inside Jack. Had he not been so certain about what he wanted out of life, the beans would have never known what to do.

Jack's story taught a great lesson to everyone who heard it: When life hands you beans, *grow a beanstalk*!

The End

LITTLE RED
RIDING HOOD

ADAPTED FROM
CHARLES PERRAULT

Once upon a time, there was a little girl who lived with her parents in a small village on the edge of the woods. She was known throughout her village as Little Red Riding Hood because of the scarlet cloak she wore around her shoulders. The cloak had been a gift from Little Red's granny, whom she loved very much.

One day, Little Red's mother received a letter from her granny. The sweet old woman was suffering from a terrible cold and couldn't leave her house, which sat a little ways into the woods. Little Red's mother packed a basket of goodies and instructed the girl to take it down the path to her grandmother's house.

"Be careful while you're in the woods, Little Red," her mother said. "Stick to the path, don't dillydally, and never talk to strangers."

Little Red took the basket and skipped down the path to her granny's house, intending to follow her mother's instructions. However, the girl had only been in the woods for a matter of moments when a field of wildflowers distracted her.

"Oh my, what beautiful flowers," Little Red said. "Surely Mother wouldn't mind if I made Granny a bouquet. Flowers help people feel better when they're ill."

She convinced herself a quick stop wouldn't hurt and had a seat in the field. Little Red picked the prettiest flowers and made herself a flower crown, a flower necklace, and two flower bracelets. By the time she finished, there were no flowers left to make a bouquet for her granny.

"Oh well," Little Red said. "I'm sure seeing me will make Granny feel just as good as a bouquet of flowers would."

Little Red returned to the path, but it wasn't long before she was distracted again. This time, a bush with vibrant blueberries caught her eye.

"Oh my, what delicious-looking berries," Little Red said. "Surely Mother wouldn't mind if I picked some for Granny. Sweets always lift someone's spirits when they're feeling under the weather."

So Little Red stopped to pick her granny some blueberries. She tested one to make sure they were sweet. She tested a second berry to make sure the first berry hadn't been a fluke. The third and fourth berries were just a little reward she gave herself for being so thoughtful.

The berries were so delicious, Little Red couldn't stop eating them. By the time she remembered to pick some for Granny, she had eaten them all.

"Oh well," Little Red said. "I'm sure I'll be as sweet a treat as anything for Granny."

Little Red didn't want to waste any more time, so she decided to stick to the path the rest of the way to her granny's house. When she was about halfway through the woods, Little Red had an awful fright. Standing on the path in front of her was a ferocious black wolf with big ears and sharp teeth.

"Hello, little girl," the wolf growled.

"Hello," Little Red said, not wanting to be rude, but then she quickly covered her mouth. "Oops—I promised my mother I wouldn't talk to strangers."

"Oh, but I'm not a stranger," the wolf said with a grin. "I've been watching you from the minute you stepped into the woods. I watched you pick flowers in the field, and I watched you eat all the blueberries off the bush. So you see, we're very well acquainted."

Little Red smiled. "Oh, that's a relief," she said. "I was afraid I had broken my word."

"What brings you into the woods, little girl?" the wolf asked.

"I'm on my way to my granny's house," Little Red said. "She's come

down with a terrible cold, so I'm bringing her a basket of goodies to cheer her up."

"What a wonderful granddaughter you are," the wolf said. "Whereabouts does your granny live?"

"Just down this path a little farther into the woods," Little Red said. "In fact, I better get going if I want to get back home in time for supper."

Little Red said good-bye to the wolf and continued her journey down the path. Unbeknownst to her, the wolf had darted through the trees beside the path and arrived at her granny's house before her. Thanks to Little Red's directions, the wolf was going to enjoy *two meals* today!

He found the old woman asleep in bed and gobbled her up in one bite. By the time Little Red arrived, the wolf was dressed in Granny's clothes and lying in her bed.

"Granny, it's Little Red," she said and knocked on the door. "I've brought you a basket of goodies!"

"Come in, my child," the wolf said, pretending to be Little Red's granny.

Little Red figured her granny must be sicker than she thought, because her voice was almost unrecognizable. She went to the side of Granny's bed and had a good look at her. The old woman didn't look like herself either.

"Oh my, what big *ears* you have," Little Red said.

"The better to *hear* you with, my dear," the wolf said.

"Oh my, what a big *nose* you have," Little Red said.

"The better to *smell* you with, my dear."

"Oh my, what sharp *teeth* you have."

"THE BETTER TO EAT YOU WITH, MY DEAR!"

The wolf leaped out from under the covers and Little Red screamed. He gobbled the little girl up in one bite, and she joined her granny in the creature's stomach. After having two meals back-to-back, the wolf was so full that he could barely move. He lay back in bed and waited for the little girl and old woman to digest.

Luckily for Little Red and her granny, a local axe man had been working in the woods nearby and heard Little Red's scream. He found Granny's house and saw that the front door was still open, so he let himself inside.

The axe man saw the wolf lying in bed with the fullest belly he had ever seen on a beast. It didn't take him long to realize what had happened. With one slice of his axe, he slew the wolf and saved Little Red and her granny from the wolf's stomach.

"Thank you so much, Mr. Axe Man," Granny said. "Little Red, what do you say to the nice man?"

Little Red didn't say a word; she had learned her lesson about talking to strangers. She ran out the door and down the path until she was safe and sound at home. Little Red never disobeyed her mother again, and because of this, she lived happily ever after.

The End

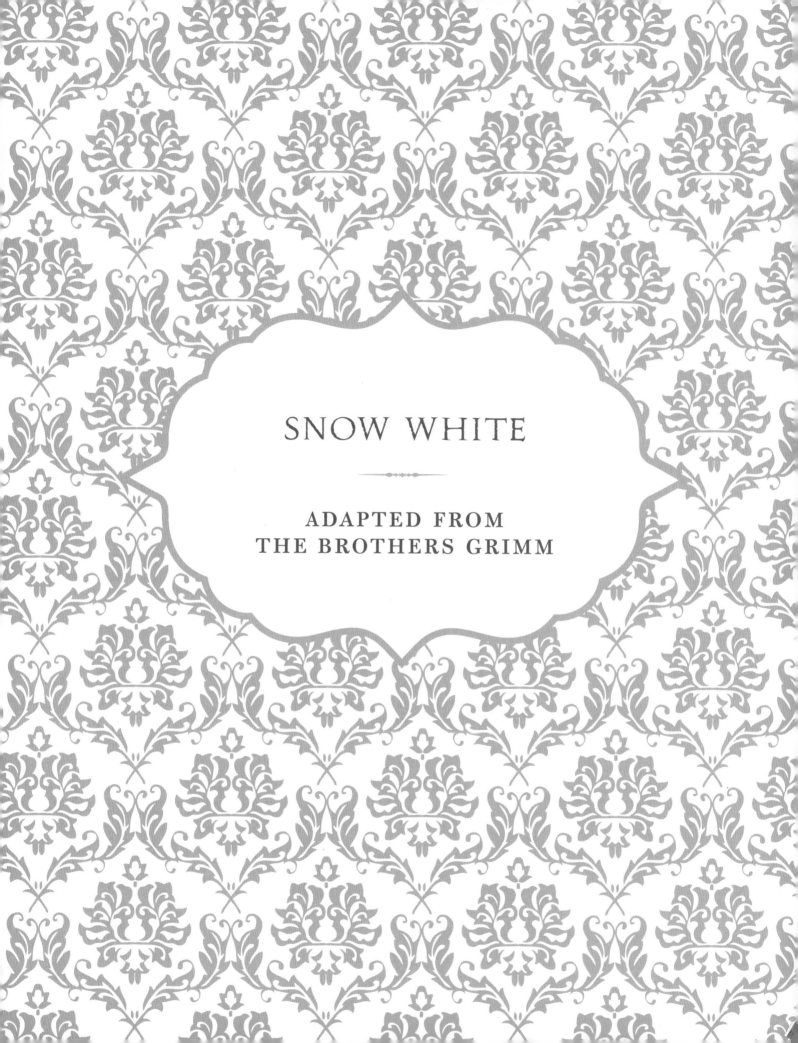

SNOW WHITE

ADAPTED FROM
THE BROTHERS GRIMM

back to his kingdom. As his traveling party continued back home, however, the wagon carrying Snow White's coffin hit a large tree root growing in the path. The motion caused a small piece of poisoned apple to come out of Snow White's mouth, and the princess awoke. The apple had not killed the princess after all, but had been lodged in her throat, causing her to fall into a deep sleep.

"Where am I?" Snow White asked.

The prince was amazed to see she was alive. He told her how he had found her in the woods and the dwarfs had let him take her so that he never had to live without her again. It was love at first sight for Snow White too, and she agreed to marry the prince.

With the help of the prince's army, Snow White returned to her castle and reclaimed her father's throne from her cruel stepmother. The Evil Queen was locked away in the dungeon without a mirror of any kind, forced to grow old without the comfort of a reflection.

The dwarfs were knighted and invited to live in the castle. Snow White became the queen of her family's kingdom, she and the prince were married, and they lived happily ever after.

The End

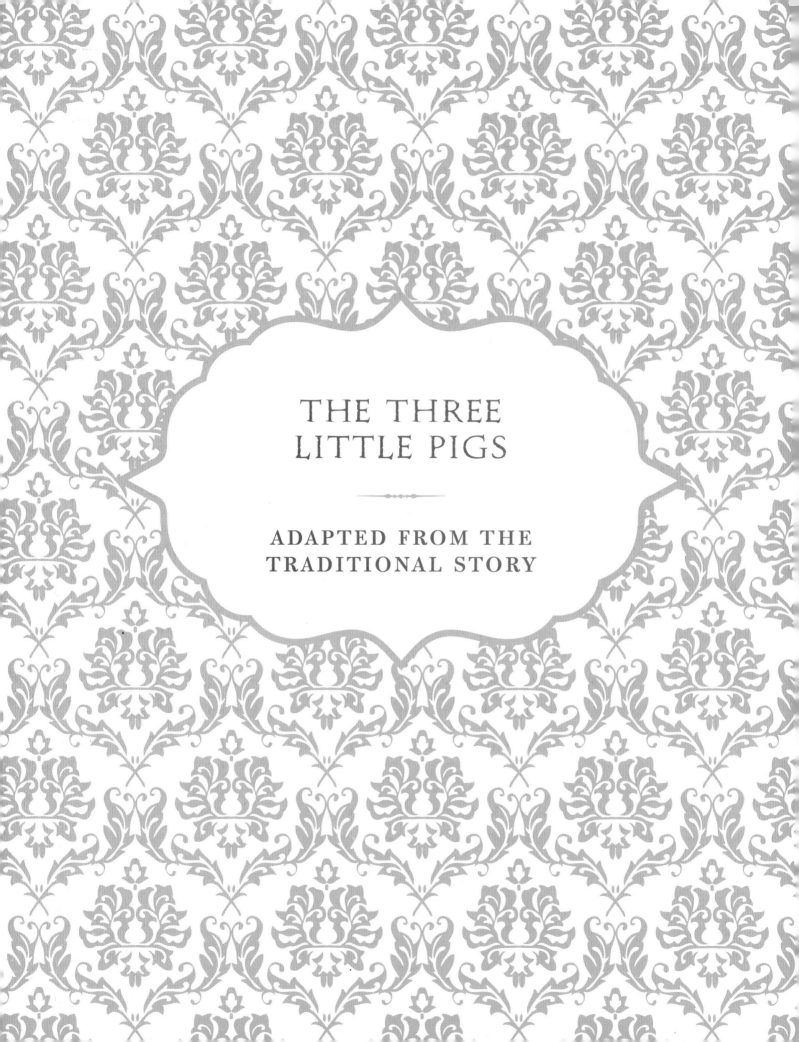

THE THREE
LITTLE PIGS

ADAPTED FROM THE
TRADITIONAL STORY

Once upon a time, there were three little pigs. Since they were no longer piglets, their mother decided it was time for them to leave the pigpen and make homes of their own. So she packed her three sons a sack of food and sent them on their way.

It may have seemed like a cruel thing for a mother to do, but the pigpen was so crowded, the three brothers were happy to leave.

The first Little Pig built his home out of straw. He thought it was a wise decision since straw was so easy to carry and assemble. It took the first Little Pig only a day to finish the straw home. It was a very flimsy house, but the Little Pig was proud of himself for completing his home so quickly.

The second Little Pig built his home out of sticks. The sticks weren't as easy to carry and assemble as straw, but they were a lot stronger. The stick house was much sturdier than his brother's straw house and it

took him only a week to build it, so the second Little Pig thought he had made a smart choice.

The third Little Pig built his home out of bricks. They were so heavy that he could only carry two at a time in his hooves, but the third Little Pig knew that bricks would make a much sturdier home than sticks and straw.

Every day on his way to the brick maker, the third Little Pig walked past his brothers' houses. They teased him mercilessly for taking on such a chore.

"You'll never finish your home!" the second Little Pig said.

"Your arms are going to fall off from carrying those bricks back and forth!" the first Little Pig said.

Despite his brothers' mean remarks, the third Little Pig knew he was doing the right thing.

"You may be laughing now, but this land is full of dangerous creatures your houses won't protect you from," the third Little Pig said.

After a tiring month, the house of bricks was finally finished.

Just as the third Little Pig had predicted, a Big Bad Wolf soon entered the land searching for his next meal. He came upon the three Little Pigs' houses and thought they would be easy catches. So he went to the house of straw first and knocked on the door.

"Little Pig, Little Pig, let me come in," the wolf called to the pig inside.

"Not by the hair on my chinny chin chin," the first Little Pig replied.

"Then I'll huff, and I'll puff, and I'll *blow your house down!*" the wolf growled.

He took a deep breath and blew the straw house away. The wolf barged inside and gobbled up the first Little Pig.

When the wolf was hungry again, he went next door to the house made of sticks and knocked on the door.

"Little Pig, Little Pig, let me come in," the wolf said.

"Not by the hair on my chinny chin chin," the second Little Pig replied.

"Then I'll huff, and I'll puff, and I'll *blow your house down!*" the wolf growled.

Just like before, the wolf took a deep breath and blew the stick house to the ground. He pounced on the second Little Pig and gobbled him up.

The wolf regained his appetite soon after and went to the house made of bricks.

"Little Pig, Little Pig, let me come in," the wolf said.

"Not by the hair on my chinny chin chin," the third Little Pig replied.

"Then I'll huff, and I'll puff, and I'll *blow your house down!*" the wolf said.

"I'd like to see you try," the third Little Pig said with a laugh.

The wolf didn't like to be mocked by his food, so this angered him very much. He took a deep breath and blew at the house. However, unlike the houses of straw and stick, the brick house stayed in one piece.

The wolf took an even deeper breath and blew at the house more strongly than before. Still, the brick house remained intact. The wolf tried again, taking the deepest breath he could and blowing it out with all his might.

Sadly for the wolf, the brick house stayed standing. He was so out of breath, the wolf fell to his knees and coughed and wheezed.

"I'll get inside your house and eat you, Little Pig, even if it's the last thing I do!" the wolf growled.

"Oh no!" the third Little Pig said. "Whatever you do, don't come through the back door!"

The wolf thought the pig was foolish for giving him such a good idea. He marched to the back of the brick house and pulled the door open. However, it wasn't an entrance to the house, but a room where the third Little Pig kept his firewood. The logs came tumbling out and piled on top of the wolf.

The third Little Pig laughed hysterically as he watched the wolf from inside. The wolf climbed out from under the pile of firewood and angrily got to his feet.

"Laugh all you want, little pig," he said. "I'll find a way inside that house and eat you just like I ate your brothers!"

"Oh no!" the third Little Pig said. "Whatever you do, don't dig a hole under the house!"

The wolf knew what the pig was doing, and he wasn't going to be fooled by it this time. He wouldn't go under the house as the pig had suggested—he was going to go *over* the house and crawl down the chimney!

The wolf fetched a ladder and climbed up to the roof of the brick house and then quickly slid down the chimney before the pig could hear him coming.

"Ready or not, here I come!" the wolf growled.

However, the third Little Pig had outsmarted the wolf again. Waiting for him at the bottom of the chimney was a large pot of boiling water. The wolf fell straight into the pot and died.

The third Little Pig added carrots and celery to the pot and cooked himself a nice wolf stew. Thanks to his wise decisions, the third Little Pig lived a long and happy life in the brick house, and remained safe from all the other wolves that came his way.

The End

Once upon a time, there was a young maiden who was the most talented spinner in her village. She lived at home with her father, who worked as a miller. The miller was so proud of his daughter, she was all he ever talked about. In fact, some of the villagers grew tired of him bragging about her.

One night, while he was getting drinks with friends at a tavern, he went on and on about how gifted his daughter was. He had been served too much and was making outlandish claims that he wouldn't have made if sober.

"My daughter is such a brilliant spinner, she could spin hay into gold!" he said.

The other men in the tavern laughed and raised their drinks to the miller and his daughter. Despite his constant boasting, it was charming to see such a supportive father.

He never expected that singing his daughter's praises would put her in harm's way. Unfortunately, one of the king's soldiers happened to also

be drinking in the tavern that night. Neither the king nor the soldier had any sense of humor whatsoever. When he heard about the maiden who could spin hay into gold, the soldier took it quite seriously. And since the kingdom was experiencing its worst financial troubles since the Dark Ages, he thought the maiden was the answer they had been looking for.

The soldier raced back to the castle and awoke the king to tell him the fortunate news.

"Your Majesty, something wonderful has happened," the soldier said. "There is a young maiden in the village who has been blessed with the power to spin hay into gold!"

"She must be a witch!" the king exclaimed. "We must arrest this woman at once and burn her at the stake!"

"Actually, Your Highness," the soldier said, "I thought a young woman like her would be most useful to the kingdom in a time like this. If she spun enough hay into gold, we would become the wealthiest nation in the world!"

"You're absolutely right," the king said. "I order you to find this maiden and bring her to the castle at once! We will put her to work straightaway!"

The soldier organized a squad and charged into the village. They knocked down the miller's door and seized the maiden. The soldiers carried her off to the castle. She was locked in a tower with nothing inside it but a spinning wheel and a stack of hay.

The maiden couldn't have been more frightened and confused. The king entered the tower, and she bowed to him.

"I beg your pardon, Your Majesty," the maiden said. "But what is the meaning of this?"

"Word of your abilities has reached the castle," the king told her. "While we should punish you for keeping such a gift from our attention, we have brought you here to redeem yourself."

"Excuse me, sir," she said. "What abilities are you referring to?"

"You have been blessed with the power of spinning hay into gold," the king said. "And now you shall do it for me."

"Your Majesty, I believe there's been some kind of mistake," the maiden said. "I am a very gifted spinner, but I most certainly cannot spin hay into—"

"Do not lie to me! We heard it from your father's lips," the king said. "You will spin the hay in this tower into gold by sunrise tomorrow morning, or your head shall be chopped off."

The king promptly turned on his heel and left. The maiden was locked in the tower alone. She fell on the floor and sobbed hysterically. It was as if she were living a nightmare. There was no way she could accomplish what the king had ordered. For all she knew, such a thing was impossible.

Just when she thought she'd most certainly lose her head, a small whirlwind spun around the tower, and a dwarf magically appeared.

"Hello, fair maiden," the dwarf said. "It seems you've found yourself in quite a predicament."

"Who are you?" she asked.

"The question isn't *who* but *what*," the dwarf said.

"Then *what* are you?"

"I may be your salvation," he said. "The king expects you to spin all the hay in this tower into gold by morning, is that correct?"

"Yes, but he is mistaken," the maiden said. "I've never been capable of such a thing. He must have misunderstood what my father said. Tomorrow morning when the king finds this tower still full of hay, I will lose my head for it."

The dwarf excitedly rubbed his hands together.

"Luckily for you, spinning hay into gold is one of my specialties. I'd be willing to help you if you'd like."

"Yes, of course!" the maiden said. "I would be so grateful!"

"I don't do anything for free," the dwarf said. "I will only spin the hay into gold if we can make a trade."

The maiden didn't have much to offer, but she was willing to trade anything if it would save her life. The dwarf looked her up and down and then side to side.

"I'll do it in exchange for your ring," he said.

It was an enchanting home with many spacious rooms and countless pieces of art on display. The merchant found a fire burning in a drawing room, which made it even more peculiar that he couldn't locate a single soul.

In the dining room, the merchant saw that the table was set for one and there were trays of hot food.

"Perhaps everyone left in a hurry," the merchant said.

Since he was starving and didn't want the food to go to waste, the merchant sat at the table and ate dinner. Once he was full, the exhaustion from his trip caught up with him, and he looked for a place to sleep.

Upstairs, the merchant found a chamber that had been prepared for a guest, as if the castle had been expecting him. He climbed into the warm bed and had a good night's sleep.

The next morning, there still was no lord or lady of the castle to be found, so the merchant left a note expressing his gratitude. He retrieved his horse from the stables and guided it away from the castle. As he went, he spotted a beautiful garden to the side of the castle containing the most gorgeous red roses he had ever seen.

"If I brought Beauty home a rose, perhaps my trip wouldn't be such a waste," he said. "At least I'll make one of my daughters happy."

The merchant went to the garden and pulled a single rose off the

bush. Suddenly, a thunderous roar came from inside the castle. The doors burst open and a hideous creature charged outside.

The Beast had the mane of a lion, the face of a bear, the horns of a goat, and the paws of a wolf. He pulled the merchant off the horse and threw him to the ground.

"I was generous enough to feed you and give you shelter for the night, and you repay me by stealing my flowers!" the Beast roared. "You did not deserve my kindness and shall pay for this!"

"Forgive me!" the merchant said. "I am very grateful to you! I would have never taken one had I known the roses were so valuable!"

"Stealing will cost you your life!" the Beast roared. "You'll never leave the castle again!"

The Beast grabbed the merchant by the collar and dragged him toward the castle.

"No, please have pity on me!" the merchant said. "I am the father of three daughters! They won't survive without me! The rose was just a gift for the youngest, Beauty."

The Beast dropped the merchant.

"Beauty, you say?" he said. "Why is she called Beauty?"

"She has the heart and face of an angel," the merchant said.

The Beast thought for a moment about the merchant and his daughter.

"You may return to your daughters," the Beast said. "But in your place, you must send Beauty to live at the castle!"

"*No!*" the merchant cried.

"Fail to do so, and I'll come for you and *all* your daughters!" he roared. "Now leave!"

The Beast threw the merchant over his horse and sent him on his way. The merchant dreaded having to tell his daughters about meeting the Beast. He worried they would have to move far away, where the creature would never find them.

When he returned home, his older daughters were so upset he didn't have any gifts for them that they locked themselves in their room and didn't come out. Beauty could see the fear in his eyes.

"Father, what's troubling you?" Beauty asked.

The merchant told his daughter about how the goods on his surviving ship had been seized to pay off his debt. He explained how he was so disheartened he became lost in the woods and found the mysterious castle. Then he told his daughter what had happened when he picked her a rose from the Beast's garden.

"It was I who asked you for a rose, and I who should pay the price for it," Beauty said. "I'll go live with the Beast in the castle so he does not harm you or my sisters."

"Absolutely not," the merchant said. "I couldn't live with myself knowing you were living with that creature! Tomorrow we will pack our things and head far away from here."

Beauty was too clever to argue with her father. Instead of fighting with him, she asked where the Beast's castle was and how to get there. The following morning, the merchant awoke to discover that Beauty was gone. Against his wishes, she had gone to live at the Beast's castle.

Beauty journeyed through the forest and into the forgotten kingdom. The castle was so tucked away, she wasn't sure she'd ever find it. Finally, looming above the trees in the distance, she saw the castle's high towers.

It was a fearful sight. The castle was much larger than she'd anticipated. She didn't know what to expect of the horrible monster waiting for her inside.

The Beast was standing at the entrance when she arrived. He was glad to see her and didn't appear as frightening to her as he had to the merchant. In fact, Beauty thought he looked rather kind.

Her beauty was well beyond what the Beast was expecting, and she took his breath away. He kneeled down and kissed her hand.

"The castle is your home now," he said. "I hope you'll find happiness here."

He led her inside, and Beauty gasped. The castle was the most

exquisite place she had ever seen. It reminded her of the home her family had lost, but it was even grander.

The Beast escorted Beauty into the dining room, where a delicious

meal was waiting on the table. At the end of the meal, the plates and silverware were cleared away magically, as if taken by invisible servants.

"The castle is enchanted with the souls of those who once worked here," the Beast said. "I apologize if it comes as a shock, but you'll get used to it."

"What's keeping the souls here?" Beauty asked.

"A curse," the Beast said, then he quickly changed the subject. "Now I'll show you to your room."

The Beast offered his arm to Beauty and walked her up a grand staircase to the upper floor. A lovely chamber had been prepared for her. So far, the Beast was a wonderful host.

In time, Beauty learned that the Beast was nothing like the vicious monster she thought he'd be. On the contrary, the longer she stayed with him, the fonder she grew of him.

Every morning, they took long walks in the garden and talked. Every evening, they would sit in the drawing room and read to each other until it was time for bed. On special occasions, the invisible servants would play instruments in the hall and Beauty and the Beast would dance.

The more time she spent at the castle, the more curious Beauty became about the castle's history. There were portraits of a handsome man hung on many of the walls, and she wondered who he was.

"Who is the man in all the paintings?" Beauty asked one night at dinner. "Did he used to live in the castle?"

"Yes, that was the prince," the Beast replied. "He hasn't lived here in many years."

Beauty was afraid to learn what happened to him, so she didn't ask any further questions. She thought of the Beast as a friend and didn't want to think he had harmed the prince in any way.

As their friendship grew, Beauty knew the Beast's feelings for her were evolving into something much more. Her suspicion turned out to be true one night when he entered her chambers and sat at the foot of her bed.

"Beauty, will you marry me?" he asked.

Beauty didn't know how to respond. She knew her answer would only hurt his feelings.

"I'm very fond of you, but I cannot marry you," she said.

The Beast nodded and left the bedroom. They went about their daily routines, and he said nothing of it for many weeks. Then one night, just like before, the Beast entered Beauty's room and sat at the foot of her bed.

"Beauty, will you marry me?" the Beast asked.

"I care very much for you, but I cannot marry you," Beauty said.

"Do you think I will ever make you happy?" the Beast asked.

"I enjoy our time together, but it's very difficult being happy here,"

Beauty said. "I miss my family more and more each day. I would do anything just to see them again."

"What if there was a way to see them without them seeing you?" the Beast asked. "Would that make you happy?"

"Oh, yes, very much!" Beauty said.

The Beast left her chambers and returned with a small hand mirror. It was a magic mirror, and all Beauty had to do was look into it and she could see her father and sisters back home at the farm. By now, both of her sisters were married, and her father was much grayer than he'd been before.

"Father is so much older now," Beauty said. "But it still brings me such joy to see they're all right!"

The Beast was pleased he could make Beauty happy. She looked into the mirror whenever she missed her family, but seeing them only made her miss them that much more. She longed to speak to them and embrace them.

One day, she saw that her father had become very ill. Her sisters and their husbands did little to care for him, and Beauty worried he would only get worse if she didn't help him.

"Beauty, why do you look so sad?" the Beast asked. "Is the mirror not working anymore?"

"My father is very sick," Beauty said. "I would do anything to go home and care for him."

The Beast knew he would regret what he was about to say, but he had fallen so in love with Beauty, he couldn't bear to see her unhappy.

"If I allow you to return home, will you promise to come back to me?" the Beast asked.

"Oh, yes!" Beauty said. "I promise to return once my father is well again!"

The Beast removed a ring from the knuckle of his paw and gave it to Beauty.

"This ring is magic," he said. "When you're ready to return, all you have to do is put it on your finger and turn the diamond three times, and you'll be back in the castle."

Beauty was so grateful, she kissed the Beast's cheek. She left the castle and hurried back to the farm. When she arrived, her father and sisters couldn't believe their eyes. They didn't think they'd ever see her again—in fact, the sisters had been hopeful they wouldn't.

"The Beast let me come home so I can take care of you, Father," Beauty said.

"He let you go?" her father asked.

"I promised him I would return once you were well," Beauty said.

"He's not as bad as he seems. I've actually grown to like him very much."

Beauty told her family about life with the Beast and all the fun things they did together. Knowing she wasn't living a miserable life made the merchant's heart warm with relief, and his health began improving immediately.

Her sisters, on the other hand, weren't happy for her at all. Beauty seemed to have a better life with the Beast than they did with their own husbands, and they became very jealous. They plotted a way to anger the Beast and sabotage their sister's happiness.

By the time her father was well, Beauty was looking forward to returning to the castle. She missed the Beast much more than she thought she would and was eager to return to their life of walks through the garden, reading in the drawing room, and dancing in the hall.

However, her sisters insisted she stay another week after their father was well. Beauty made it very clear that she had promised the Beast she would return as soon as their father was healthy again, but her sisters were so persistent, Beauty agreed to stay just a few days longer.

What Beauty didn't know was that, at that exact moment, the Beast was watching her through the magic mirror. Watching her break her promise broke the Beast's heart. He knew she would never love him as much as he loved her.

When it was finally time to leave the farm, Beauty placed the magic ring on her finger and turned the diamond three times. She was magically transported back to the castle and sighed with relief. The castle now felt more like home than the farmhouse did.

"I'm back," Beauty called through the halls, but she couldn't find the Beast anywhere. "Where are you?"

Beauty passed a window and screamed. In the garden she saw the Beast lying on the ground under the rosebush. He was as still as stone, and his paw was clutching his chest. It appeared the Beast had died of a broken heart waiting for Beauty to return.

She ran out into the garden and collapsed on top of him. Tears ran down her face, and she rested her head above his heart.

"Please don't die," she cried. "While I was away, I realized just how much I care for you. I love you with my whole heart. Nothing would make me happier than to marry you."

A sudden gust of wind surrounded them. Beauty looked up to see what was happening, and when she looked down, the Beast was gone. A handsome man had taken his place.

"Beauty, you've come back!" the man said.

She recognized the man—he was the prince from all the paintings throughout the castle.

When it was finally time to leave the farm, Beauty placed the magic ring on her finger and turned the diamond three times. She was magically transported back to the castle and sighed with relief. The castle now felt more like home than the farmhouse did.

"I'm back," Beauty called through the halls, but she couldn't find the Beast anywhere. "Where are you?"

Beauty passed a window and screamed. In the garden she saw the Beast lying on the ground under the rosebush. He was as still as stone, and his paw was clutching his chest. It appeared the Beast had died of a broken heart waiting for Beauty to return.

She ran out into the garden and collapsed on top of him. Tears ran down her face, and she rested her head above his heart.

"Please don't die," she cried. "While I was away, I realized just how much I care for you. I love you with my whole heart. Nothing would make me happier than to marry you."

A sudden gust of wind surrounded them. Beauty looked up to see what was happening, and when she looked down, the Beast was gone. A handsome man had taken his place.

"Beauty, you've come back!" the man said.

She recognized the man—he was the prince from all the paintings throughout the castle.

"You're the prince!" she asked. "But where's the Beast?"

"I am the Beast," the prince said happily. "Many years ago, an evil Enchantress thought I was too vain and needed to be taught a lesson. She cursed me to look like a beast and cursed the souls of my servants to stay trapped in the castle. The only way to break the spell was to be loved by someone of true beauty!"

With the curse lifted, the souls of the servants trapped in the castle were freed. Beauty and the prince were married and became rulers of the forgotten kingdom. The merchant joined them at the castle, leaving his selfish daughters behind, and they all lived happily ever after.

The End

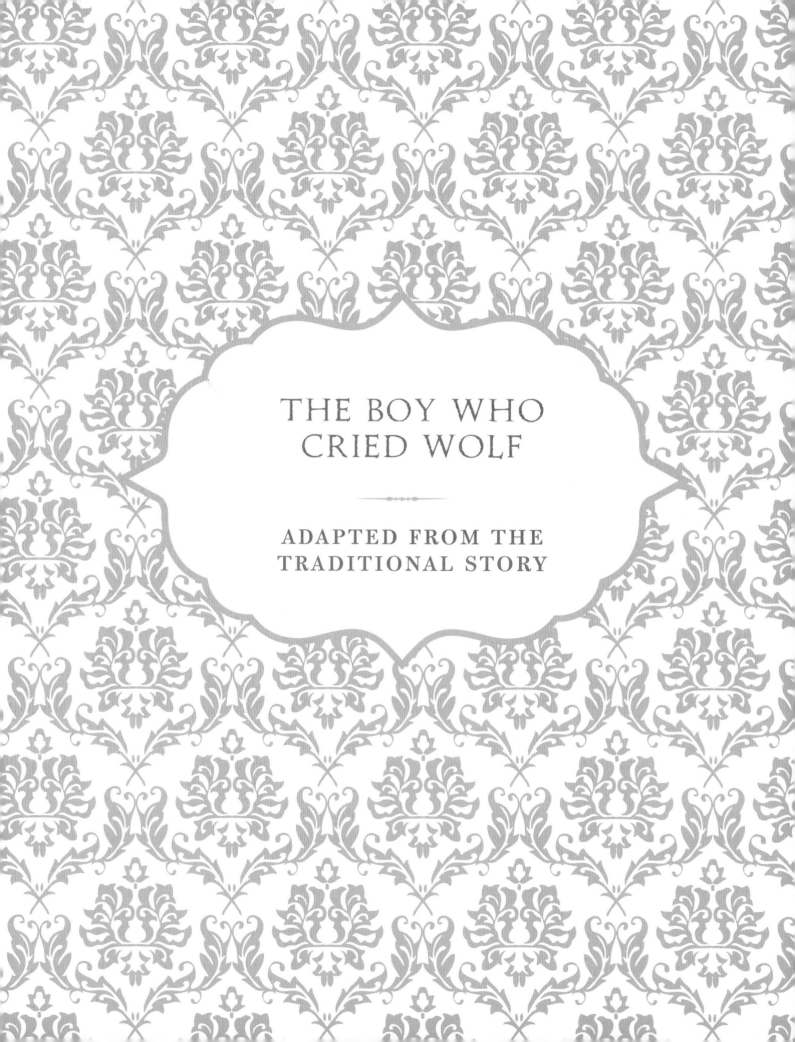

THE BOY WHO
CRIED WOLF

ADAPTED FROM THE
TRADITIONAL STORY

Once upon a time, there was a little boy who lived on a farm with his family. They were an organized bunch, and each family member had his or her own set of chores to keep the farm running.

His father farmed all the crops and sold them in the local village. His mother cooked and cleaned and made sure everyone else was pulling his or her own weight. His brothers fed the chickens and the pigs and kept the pigpens and henhouses clean. His sisters milked the cows and goats and carefully kept track of which milk was which.

Being the youngest in his family, the little boy was given the simplest task on the farm. Every day, he would take the farm's herd of sheep into a field nearby and look after them as they grazed on the grass. At night, when his mother rang the bell for supper, he'd escort the sheep back into their pen, and the whole thing would start over again the next day.

It was such an easy chore that the little boy spent most of the day being bored and restless. Even with a good imagination, it was difficult to keep himself entertained in the field.

He'd practice balancing his straw hat on the end of his staff, but he grew tired of that. He'd look for anthills and stomp on them until all the ants came out, but that got old pretty quick. He'd build buildings out of rocks, but eventually he ran out of rocks.

One afternoon, after he had done everything he could think of to pass the time, he decided to play a joke on his family.

"Wolf!" he cried. *"There's a wolf in the field!"*

His father and his brothers immediately came running from the farm with their pitchforks and axes raised high. His mother and sisters ran out too, swinging rolling pins and carving knives. However, when they arrived in the field, there wasn't a wolf anywhere.

The little boy burst into a fit of giggles.

"I tricked you!" he laughed. "There's no wolf out here! You should have seen the looks on your faces!"

His siblings rolled their eyes and went back to the farm. His parents shook their heads and scowled at him. The little boy figured he was the only one in his family who had a sense of humor.

The next day, the little boy was back in the field watching over the flock of sheep as always. He was so bored, he didn't know what to do with himself.

He practiced twirling his staff, but it kept hitting him in the head. He laid on the grass and thought about what the clouds were shaped like, but there were only one or two in the sky that day. He tried teaching the sheep tricks, like how to fetch and roll over, but the sheep weren't interested in learning.

Finally, he was so desperate for excitement that he decided to play another joke on his family.

"Wolf!" he cried. *"There's a wolf in the field!"*

Just like the day before, his family ran toward the field with pitch-forks, axes, rolling pins, and knives raised. But before they reached the field, the little boy fell and rolled on the ground with bellyache-inducing laughter.

"I tricked you again!" he said with a giggle.

His parents and siblings were at their wit's end with him. Even the sheep were annoyed, because the little boy frightened them each time he yelled.

"I'm glad you're pleased with yourself, because the rest of us sure aren't!" his father said. "Scare us like that again and you'll get a whipping."

The little boy was so tickled with himself, he laughed until it was time to head back for supper. Unfortunately, the next day the joke was on him.

Just like always, the little boy was back in the field watching the sheep. He was walking around looking for something to do, when out of the corner of his eye he saw a frightening sight. At the edge of the field was a pack of enormous wolves.

They had thick, matted fur, long claws, and razor-sharp teeth. Their mouths watered, and they licked their lips as they watched the little boy and his herd.

The sheep saw the wolves and quickly ran from the field, causing a small stampede. The little boy was left all alone, and the wolves began circling him. He was so scared, he froze where he stood and it took him a few moments before he was able to make a sound.

"*Wolves!*" he cried. "*There are wolves in the field!*"

However, his family didn't come.

"*Wolves!*" he cried louder. "*There are wolves in the field! A whole pack of them!*"

Still, no one from the farm came to save him.

"*WOLVES!*" the boy cried as loud as he could. "*Come quick before they eat me!*"

His family heard him loud and well, but they thought he was only trying to trick them again. They shook their heads and continued their own chores.

The wolves pounced on the little boy and gobbled him up. The family didn't realize what had happened until suppertime, when the boy didn't return from watching the sheep. They went to the field to see what was keeping him, but all that was left was his staff and straw hat.

Naturally, it was devastating for the family and all the villagers who knew him. With the family's permission, the village built a monument for the little boy in the center of town. It reminded the other children in the village the importance of honesty and having an honorable reputation. Even little white lies can cause big trouble.

The End

SLEEPING BEAUTY

ADAPTED FROM
CHARLES PERRAULT

Once upon a time, in a far-off land, there lived a sad queen who could not have children. Although she had every luxury imaginable, the one thing she wanted more than anything was a child to hold in her arms. She cried herself to sleep every night knowing she would never be a mother. The king did everything he could to make his wife happy, but nothing eased the queen's heartbreak.

One afternoon, to take her mind off the unfortunate matter, the queen took a walk beside a river. She stopped for a moment when she noticed something strange; it was a large fish flopping on the riverbank. Although her heart was broken, it still was kind, so the queen helped the poor fish back into the water. To her surprise, the fish peeked its head out of the water and began talking.

"Thank you ever so much for helping me back into the river," the fish said. "I jumped out of the water to escape a predator, but I would have suffocated on the bank if it hadn't been for you."

"Oh my! You can speak?" the queen asked.

"I can, because I'm a magic fish," he said. "I am so grateful to you for saving my life. I would like to say thank you by granting you a wish, if you'll allow it. Although I'm sure a queen as fair as you does not want for much."

At first the queen thought she might be ill or dreaming. She had never heard of a talking fish before—let alone one that could grant her magic wishes. But just in case she was not ill and was not dreaming, the sad queen told the fish her heart's greatest desire.

"I wish to have a child," the queen said. "But if that's too big of a wish for a fish to grant, I understand."

The fish winked both eyes at her, and the wish was granted.

"Nine months from now, you will be blessed with a child," it said and swam away.

True to his word, nine months later the queen gave birth to a baby girl. It was such a miracle, the king hosted a giant celebration for everyone in the kingdom to welcome his child into the world.

There were parades and fireworks, singing and dancing, and costumes and games. The rulers from neighboring and distant lands came to join the festivities. Fairies visited the castle to bestow gifts upon the infant princess.

One fairy blessed the princess with the gift of beauty. Another fairy

blessed her with the gift of health. The princess was also blessed with the gifts of talent, intelligence, and grace. Finally, it was the smallest fairy's turn to bless her. She flew up to the cradle and withdrew her wand.

"Sweet baby princess, the gift I would like to leave you with is the gift of—"

Unfortunately, before the smallest fairy had her chance to bless the princess, she was interrupted. An evil Enchantress stormed the castle, and the celebration came to a halt.

The Enchantress was a terrible and cruel woman. She was the only person in all the kingdom not to have received an invitation, and when she'd learned this, it had angered her beyond reason.

"You have no business being here!" the king yelled. "Leave at once!"

"Leave?" the Enchantress said. "I didn't come all this way for nothing. I *too* have a gift for the child."

Everyone in attendance gasped, for they knew that the Enchantress's gift for the princess would be very unpleasant.

"Please don't, I beg of you!" the queen said. "She's our only child!"

But before she could be convinced otherwise, the evil Enchantress had already begun. She didn't bestow a gift on the baby princess, but a nasty curse.

"The child shall indeed grow to be beautiful, wise, and graceful,"

Once upon a time, there lived a baker and his wife. They lived above their bakery in a small village, next door to a mysterious vegetable garden. The garden had thick brick walls built on all four sides to protect its vegetables from pests.

In all their time living above the bakery, the baker and his wife never met the owner of the garden, nor did they see anyone going in or out of it. However, from the window of their bedroom, they could peer down into it and gawk at all the delicious crops growing between the walls.

The tomatoes were bright red and ripe, the cabbage was healthy and full, and the mushrooms were plump and lush. Sadly, no one ever seemed to enjoy the vegetables growing there. The crops always rotted back into the earth before being eaten.

The baker and his wife had much more important things to worry about than the neglected garden; they were expecting their first child.

While carrying the baby, the wife was experiencing the strongest

cravings she had ever felt. Being a good husband, the baker happily fetched his wife whatever it was she wanted to eat.

One day, the wife's hungry gaze fell upon the lettuce in their neighbor's garden. They were some of the juiciest greens she had ever seen. Day and night she dreamed about making a salad or stew out of the leaves. The wife's craving for the lettuce increased every day, until she almost died from desire.

"Oh, darling, I would love nothing more than to have a bite of the delicious lettuce in our neighbor's garden," she said. "Would you mind climbing the wall and bringing me back some?"

"You want me to steal from our neighbor, my dear?" the baker asked.

"It'll only go to waste if we don't eat it," the wife said. "Besides, we've never seen so much as a mouse next door! No one will ever know."

The baker was hesitant at first, but he was willing to do anything to be a good father and husband. He figured some mild thievery wouldn't harm anyone.

As soon as the sun set that night, the baker climbed the wall into his neighbor's garden and brought back some lettuce for his wife. She cooked it, and the happy couple enjoyed it for dinner without a care in the world. Little did they know that stealing the lettuce would be the biggest mistake of their lives.

Unbeknownst to the baker and his wife, the garden next door

belonged to a terrible witch, who noticed that the head of lettuce was missing as soon as it was taken. She barged into the baker's home and caught him and his wife eating it.

"Thieves!" the witch yelled. "How dare you steal from me! I'll curse you for this!"

The baker and his wife fell to their knees and begged the witch for forgiveness.

"We're so sorry!" the baker said. "We've never seen the crops in your garden harvested before!"

"We didn't know the lettuce would be missed!" the wife said.

"Fools!" the witch roared. "The vegetables in my garden are not meant for eating—*they're meant for making potions!* The lettuce you stole from me is called *rapunzel*. When it's prepared correctly, it will bring hair back to the bald or sight back to the blind!"

"Please take something of ours in exchange," the baker said.

"Yes, anything you'd like!" the wife said. "But please don't curse us!"

The witch was looking forward to putting a curse on their house, but their offer was very intriguing.

"Anything I'd like, you say?" she asked.

"Yes, anything!" the baker and his wife said together.

The witch looked around their tiny home. She didn't find anything that interested her until her eyes fell upon the wife's pregnant belly. A

child was something the witch had never owned before, so it was an easy decision.

"I shall return when you give birth, and your *child* shall be mine!" the witch declared.

"No!" the baker pleaded. *"Anything but our child!"*

"Do not argue with me!" the witch warned. "You will hand the child over to me, or I will curse you into oblivion!"

Two months later, the wife gave birth to a beautiful and healthy baby girl. She had been in her mother's arms for only a few short moments when the witch returned. Although every fiber of his being urged him not to, the baker handed his newborn daughter over to her.

"I shall name her *Rapunzel*, so what you *stole* and what was *stolen* from you shall always be one and the same," the witch said.

She disappeared with the child, and the baker and his wife never saw her again.

The witch took the child into the middle of the woods and locked her away in the room of a very tall tower where no one could reach her. There were no doors or stairs in the tower, just a single small window, so the witch had to climb the tower brick by brick every day when she visited.

As the witch got older, this became a much harder and harder task, but an alternative method presented itself when Rapunzel grew into a young woman.

Thanks to the magic of the lettuce her mother had consumed, Rapunzel's hair grew faster, longer, and stronger than that of all the other maidens in the land put together. When the witch came for a visit, she would call up to the tower:

"Rapunzel, Rapunzel, let down your hair!"

Rapunzel would lower her hair, and the witch would climb it as if it were rope.

Every day during the witch's visit, Rapunzel would ask her the same question.

"Mother," Rapunzel called the witch, for she had never known any other. "One day, when I am older and wiser, will you let me down from this tower so I may explore the world?"

"Absolutely not," the witch replied. "The world is a dark and cruel place, my dear. You're much better off staying here where it's safe."

"But I get so lonely in this tower all by myself," Rapunzel said.

"My dear, *greed* is your problem, not *loneliness*," the witch said. "There are maidens in this world with far less than you. They would be happy to have the protection of this tower. I will not hear any more of this nonsense. You should be grateful for the life I've given you."

Despite what the witch said, this daily exchange didn't make Rapunzel more grateful, only more curious. She didn't believe the world was as bad as the witch made it seem. She spent all day gazing at the woods around her, dreaming about what it was like outside her tower.

Rapunzel prayed every day that she would find a way to leave the tower and have someone to leave it with. Soon, an answer to her prayer arrived…but she didn't find it—it found her.

A handsome young man was wandering through the forest when he discovered Rapunzel's tower in the woods. He was a curious person himself and circled the base of the tower to find a way inside.

The witch arrived for her daily visit with Rapunzel, and the young man hid from her behind a thornbush. He watched as she called up to the tower:

"Rapunzel, Rapunzel, let down your hair!"

Rapunzel appeared in the window and dropped her hair for the witch to climb. The young man's heart raced upon seeing her. He had

never seen a girl as beautiful as she, and he wanted nothing more than to climb up the tower and meet her.

He waited outside the tower and listened to Rapunzel and the witch's conversation. It was the same as it was every day: Rapunzel's requests to leave the tower were dismissed by the witch, who told her how ungrateful she was for asking.

The young man was compelled to save poor Rapunzel from the tower and the witch. The next day he returned to the tower with a plan to meet her. He waited for the witch to arrive and hid from view as she called up to the tower:

"Rapunzel, Rapunzel, let down your hair!"

The hair was lowered and the witch climbed it to the window. The witch and the young woman had the same conversation as always, and when they had finished, the witch climbed down Rapunzel's hair and left the tower for her home in the village.

The young man waited until he was certain the witch was gone and then called up to the tower himself:

"Rapunzel, Rapunzel, let down your hair!"

The witch had never visited Rapunzel twice in one day. Fearing something was wrong, Rapunzel quickly lowered her hair for the caller. She never had any other guests besides the witch, so it gave her quite a scare to see the young man climb through the window.

"Who are you?" she asked.

"Don't worry, I will not harm you," he said. "Forgive me, but I saw you in this tower yesterday, and I had to meet you."

"Where are you from?" Rapunzel asked.

"The village at the edge of the woods," he said.

"There's a *village* at the edge of the woods?" Rapunzel said, and her eyes grew wide at the idea. "Please, you must tell me all about it!"

The young man told Rapunzel everything there was to know about his village. He told her about all the roads, shops, markets, houses, and schools. He told her about his family and his friends and how they treated one another so differently than the witch treated her.

"How wonderful," Rapunzel said with a dreamy sigh.

"There's a lot more I'd like to tell you," the young man said. "May I come back and visit you again?"

"I would love that," Rapunzel said.

Every day from then on, once the witch had come and gone, the young man would climb up Rapunzel's hair and visit her in the tower. Each day he would bring new things to show her about the world outside.

He showed her maps of his village, maps of the forest, maps of the kingdom, and maps of the known world. He brought her books and scrolls so she could read about all the places and people she never knew existed.

"If only I could leave this tower and see the world with my own eyes," Rapunzel said desperately.

"I'll help you leave the tower so we can travel the world together," the young man said.

"But what about my mother?" Rapunzel asked. "She'd be heartbroken if I left."

"A real mother doesn't keep her child locked away in a tower," he said. "A real mother would want you to leave and have experiences. She'd want you to live, learn, and *love*."

And with that said, the young man kissed Rapunzel. For the first time in her life, Rapunzel felt like a person and not a prisoner. She decided to leave the tower, even if it was the last thing she did.

"How will I get down without Mother noticing?" she said.

"Leave it to me," the young man said. "I'll come up with something so the witch will never be the wiser."

From that day forward, when the young man visited the tower he brought Rapunzel handfuls of twine the same color as her hair. She would twist the twine into rope and then braid the rope into her hair, so the witch never found it. Once the rope was as long as her hair, Rapunzel planned to use it to climb down from the tower and be free.

At the time, it seemed like the perfect plan. The longer the rope became, the more Rapunzel's and the young man's excitement grew.

However, their excitement made them careless, and one afternoon the young man foolishly left one of his maps behind.

The witch found the map and screamed at Rapunzel.

"Tell me who's been visiting you!" she demanded.

"No," Rapunzel said with a quivering jaw.

"Tell me now, or I will curse them when I find out who they are!" the witch warned.

"Just a young man from the village at the edge of the woods," Rapunzel said. "Is it so wrong to have a friend?"

Rapunzel burst into tears. The witch had never seen her so sad before. It was the first time the witch felt sorry for the girl, and she kneeled down to comfort her. However, all the witch's guilt quickly diminished when she stroked Rapunzel's head and found the rope braided into her hair.

"*You horrible, ungrateful girl!*" the witch yelled. "*After everything I've done for you, you were going to leave the tower and run off with that scoundrel! I'll make sure you never see each other again!*"

The witch left the tower and returned with an axe and a rope ladder. She chopped off all of Rapunzel's hair with the axe and then forced her down the ladder. The witch dragged the poor girl into the forest and abandoned her at a spot so deep in the woods, she would never find her way back.

The witch returned to the tower, discarded the ladder and the axe in the shrubbery below, and waited for the young man to arrive the next day. For all he knew, Rapunzel would be freed soon, so there was an extra bounce in his step. He stood at the base of the tower and called up:

"Rapunzel, Rapunzel, let down your hair!"

The witch let down Rapunzel's hair for the young man to climb. When he reached the very top of the tower, she pulled it out of his hands and knocked him off the window ledge.

The thornbush below broke his fall, but the thorns pierced his eyes and blinded him. The young man wandered into the wilderness, not knowing in which direction he was headed.

For months and months, the young man wandered the forest blindly. Every day he called for help until his voice grew hoarse, but no one ever heard him.

Miraculously, the young man and Rapunzel found each other in the woods, but she wasn't alone. Since they had been separated, Rapunzel had given birth to twins.

"You're a father," she told him. "We can be a family now."

The young man cried tears of both joy and pain. He was happy to have a family, but he knew he would never lay eyes on them. Rapunzel rested his head in her lap and cried with him. Her tears rolled down her face and fell into his eyes.

to feet, her scales turned to skin, and two wonderful legs appeared on her body.

The Little Mermaid—no longer a mermaid—almost drowned in the Sea Witch's cave. She swam to the ocean surface just before it was too late and washed ashore on the beach in the exact spot she had left the prince.

Luckily, the prince himself returned to this beach every day hoping to find answers to the mystery of his rescue. He found the Little Mermaid and helped her to her feet. Since she had never walked before, she immediately fell back on the ground.

"What happened to you?" the prince asked.

The Little Mermaid tried to respond, but without a tongue, she could only mumble.

"What's your name?" the prince asked.

Again, the Little Mermaid tried to tell him, but he didn't understand.

"You don't talk much, do you?" the prince said with a smile. "Why don't I take you home to my castle and get you cleaned up?"

The Little Mermaid nodded her head, and tears came to her eyes. She couldn't imagine anything more wonderful than that. She stayed with the prince for many months, and he took wonderful care of her.

The prince taught the Little Mermaid how to walk, how to run,

and how to dance. They danced together every night before bed, each night dancing closer and closer, until they were so close she could rest her head on his chest and they swayed as one.

The Little Mermaid was convinced the prince loved her as much as she loved him. The transformation was worth every ounce of pain.

One day, a beautiful young woman arrived at the castle accompanied by the sound of trumpets and cheering crowds. From the look on the Little Mermaid's face, the prince knew she didn't recognize the young woman.

"She's a princess from another kingdom and my *betrothed*," he said. "We're going to be married at the end of the week."

The Little Mermaid collapsed on the ground when she heard this. She felt as if her heart had broken into a dozen pieces.

"I'm sorry, I thought you knew," the prince said. "I thought everyone in the kingdom knew."

The Little Mermaid ran from the castle in tears. Knowing the prince loved someone else gave her the strongest pain she had ever felt. She headed for the ocean and fell to her knees on the sand.

Just as she was about to touch the water with her toe and become sea foam, all five of her sisters surfaced in the water ahead.

"Dear sister, we've been looking everywhere for you!" the oldest said.

Something was different about the Mer princesses. When the Little Mermaid took a closer look, she saw that all of their beautiful hair had been chopped off.

"What happened to your hair?" she mumbled, and thankfully her sisters understood what she meant.

"We've traded it to the Sea Witch in hopes of turning you back into a mermaid," the second oldest said. "She gave us this dagger and said if you want to return to the sea, you must stab the prince in the heart with it and let the blood fall on your feet."

The second oldest placed a small dagger with a blade of sea glass and a handle of coral at the Little Mermaid's feet.

The Little Mermaid returned to the castle on the night of the prince's wedding. She snuck through the halls and entered the newly-weds' chambers. She stood over the prince and raised the dagger above his heart.

Right as she was about to strike, the Little Mermaid froze. She looked down at the prince as he slept peacefully beside his new bride and realized she could never cause him harm. Although the prince did not love her, she still loved him very much.

The Little Mermaid returned to the beach and threw the dagger into the ocean. She stepped into the cold water and walked into the sea toward the full moon. As much as I'd like to say the Little Mermaid

had a happily-ever-after, her body turned into sea foam just as the Sea Witch had warned her.

However, she did not cease to exist as she had been told. The Little Mermaid's spirit lived on, traveling across the ocean to help those in need and guiding young people away from making mistakes similar to her own.

The End

THREE
BILLY GOATS GRUFF

ADAPTED FROM
ASBJØRNSEN & MOE

Once upon a time, there was a family of three billy goats who lived together in a field. The goats were brothers and were different in size and age. The youngest was the smallest and had only the slightest hint of horns growing on his head. The second-oldest goat was larger and had much bigger horns than his younger brother. The oldest brother was the largest goat in the family and had two strong horns growing on top of his head.

One day, the family of goats ran out of grass to eat in their field. It wasn't a problem, though, because there happened to be another grassy field just on the other side of the river. So the goats traveled down the river until they found a small stone bridge.

The youngest goat crossed the bridge first. Before he made it to the other side, a hideous troll jumped up from under the bridge and blocked his path.

"How dare you cross my bridge without paying the toll?" the troll roared.

The little goat trembled in the troll's presence.

"I'm sorry, Mr. Troll," he said. "But I'm only a goat and have no gold coins to spare."

"Then you shall be my dinner!" the troll growled, and lunged toward the frightened goat.

"Wait!" the goat said. "I would make you nothing but a small snack. You should wait until my older brother crosses your bridge and eat him. He'll make you a much more satisfying meal!"

The troll couldn't believe the small goat would wish this upon his own brother, but he had a point. He let the little goat pass and waited for his brother to cross the bridge.

"How dare you cross my bridge without paying the toll?" the troll roared.

"I'm sorry, sir!" said the second-oldest goat. "But I am just a simple billy goat and have no money to give."

"Then you shall be my dinner!" the troll growled.

"Wait!" the goat said. "I would only be a light meal for you, but if you wait for my older and larger brother to cross your bridge, you'll have a wonderful feast!"

The goats were the most dysfunctional family the troll had ever

Once upon a time, there lived two princesses in a stunning castle. Even though they shared the same parents, the same home, and led similar lives, the sisters couldn't have been more different.

The older sister was a mean and selfish girl. She called the castle servants horrible names and threw tantrums whenever she didn't get her way. The younger sister was sweet and kind. She had a big heart and was nice to everyone she met.

One day, the older sister took a stroll through the castle gardens by herself. She was playing with her favorite toy, a small sphere made of pure gold. The princess practiced tossing it into the air and catching it. She accidently dropped it into a small pond, and it sank to the bottom.

"Oh no!" the older sister said. "I'll never retrieve it!"

Right when she turned to head back to the castle, a frog leaped out of the pond clutching the golden ball in his mouth.

"Hello, princess," he said. "I believe this belongs to you."

"That was nice of you," she said. "Is there anything I could give you in return? A soft lily pad to lie on or a nice jar of flies?"

"Actually, there is something you could give me, something I desire very much," the frog said. "A *kiss* would be much appreciated."

The older princess was disgusted that the frog would request something so disturbing. To teach him a lesson, she picked him up by the leg and threw him against a brick wall in the garden.

"How dare you ask such a thing from a princess," she said and walked away.

The younger princess had been watching the whole thing from a tower. She hurried outside to see if the frog was hurt.

"You poor thing," the younger princess said. "I'm terribly sorry she did that to you. Will you be all right?"

"Oh, yes, I'll be perfectly fine," the frog said.

"My sister can be cruel," she said. "Perhaps I could make it up to you. I'd be delighted to give you a kiss."

The younger princess placed the frog in the palm of her hand and raised him up to her face. She kissed the frog's lips and set him back on the ground.

"There you are," she said. "I hope you have a lovely—"

Suddenly, the frog began to twist and turn; he shimmied and he shook. His body stretched to ten times his size, and his green skin peeled away. The frog magically transformed into the handsomest young man the young princess had ever seen.

"Good heavens!" the young princess gasped. *"You're a man?"*

"Indeed," he said. "I was once the prince of a powerful kingdom,

until an evil witch cursed me to live as a frog. She said the only way to break the spell was to receive a kiss from a princess."

The young princess and the prince traveled across the land to his home, and the kingdom rejoiced at his return. The prince and the younger princess were married and eventually became the king and queen.

The older princess stayed at home and spent the rest of her life kissing every frog and toad she could find. However, none of them turned into a handsome prince. She never found a husband, but she did receive many warts.

The End

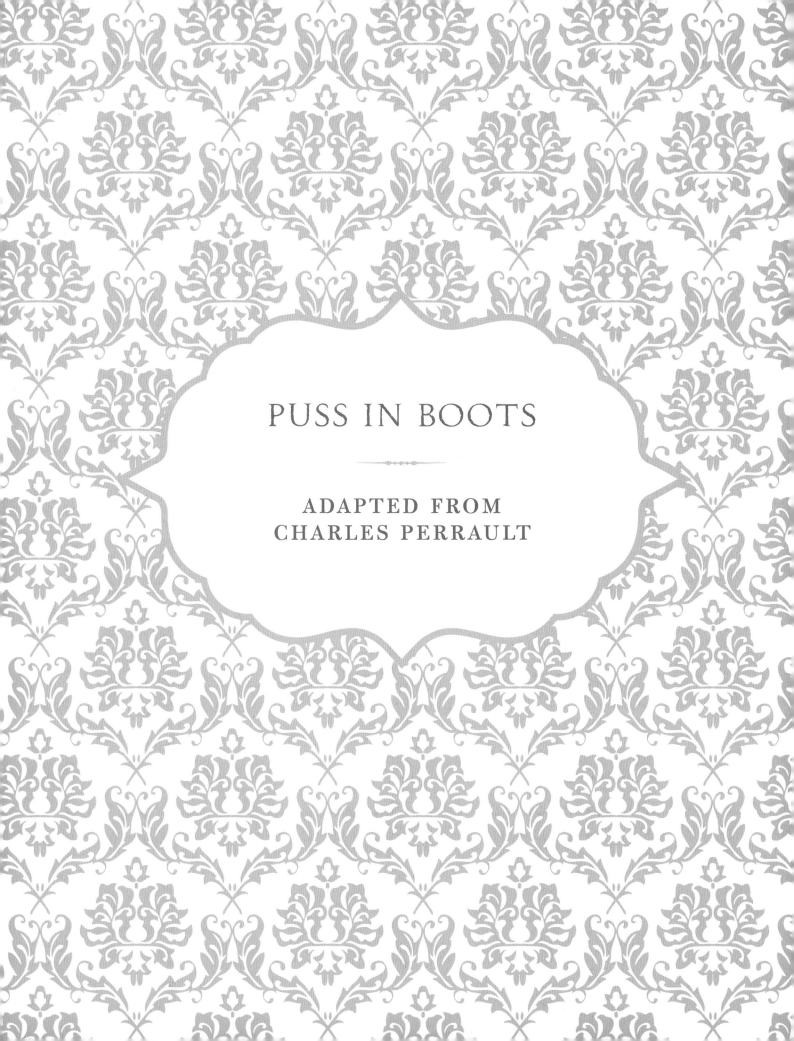

PUSS IN BOOTS

ADAPTED FROM
CHARLES PERRAULT

Once upon a time, there was a miller who had three sons. Just before he died, the miller wrote a will so there would be no confusion over where he wished his possessions to go.

The oldest son received the mill, so he could continue his father's work. The middle son received all the horses and animals, so he could start a farm of his own. The youngest son, who was named John, inherited his father's cat.

At first, John felt snubbed by the inheritance. He loved his father very much and had always been good to him. John didn't understand why his father would leave his brothers so much and him so little.

What John didn't know yet was that the cat happened to be his father's most prized possession. He knew John and the cat would accomplish great things together.

The cat in question was named Puss. He was a brown tabby with

green eyes and black stripes. He was a conniving little fellow and by far the smartest cat in the land.

"Looks like I'm stuck with you, kitty," John said with a sigh.

"I'm not thrilled about this either," Puss said. "After all the mice I caught and the snuggles I gave your father, I can't believe he left me with *you*."

"You can talk?" John said.

"I've always talked, you've just never listened," Puss said. "Now listen to this: Your father obviously put us together for a reason. We might as well make the most of it. I've put together a plan that will make us rich!"

The cat definitely had John's attention. "What's your plan?"

"Part of my plan is never speaking of my plan," the cat said. "But I will need your absolute trust and cooperation if it's going to work."

John didn't have anything better to do, and he figured any plan was better than no plan at all.

"I'm here for whatever you need," he said.

"Good," Puss said. "First, I will need you to take me into town to purchase a new wardrobe. I must look my best for the first step of the plan."

John and Puss went into town and shopped at the fanciest stores in the village. Puss purchased tall leather boots, a smart feathered hat, and a long silver sword. It cost John every penny he had.

"Are you positive you need such fancy things?" John said. "There are plenty of cheaper options."

"Sometimes you've got to spend what you're looking to earn," Puss said. "Besides, I will need to look presentable for the king."

"The *king*?" John said. "You didn't tell me your plan involved the king!"

"That's because you never asked," the cat said. "Now we must gather some carrots and go into the woods."

They stole carrots from a farmer's garden and then traveled into the forest. They laid the carrots out on the ground and waited behind a tree.

"What are we doing?" John asked.

"Step two, *hunting*," Puss replied.

Just then, a plump rabbit climbed out from its hole in the ground and began eating the carrots. Puss snuck up behind it and snapped its neck.

The following day, Puss traveled to the king's castle wearing his new clothes. A talking cat in high boots and a hat was such an odd sight, none of the king's men stopped him from going inside. Puss walked right into the throne room and laid the rabbit down at the king's feet.

"A gift for His Majesty, from my master," the cat said and bowed.

The king was just as surprised as anyone to see him.

"You can talk?" he said.

"Of course I can talk," Puss said. "I imagine His Majesty is so magnificent, most animals are speechless around him."

This answer pleased the king greatly, and he smiled down at the charming cat.

"Who did you say this was from?" the king asked.

"My master, the great Marquis of Carabas," Puss said. "Your Majesty is so well traveled, I'm positive you know him."

The king did not recall such a man, but he pretended to be familiar with him so he wasn't embarrassed in front of his court. Besides, he had met so many people throughout the kingdom, it was possible they were acquainted.

"Of course, the Marquis of Carabas," the king said. "Please thank your master kindly for me."

Puss bowed again and left the castle. With step three of his plan a success, he immediately went on to step four.

Every Sunday afternoon, the king enjoyed a carriage ride through the kingdom with his daughter, the princess. Puss was fully aware of this and planned to take advantage of the king's routine. He took John to a lake on the edge of the road he knew the king's carriage would travel down.

"Now take off all your clothes and get in the lake," Puss said.

"Do *what*?" John said. "How on earth is that going to help us get rich?"

"We don't have time to argue; the king is on his way!" Puss said. "Quickly, undress and get into the lake."

John was starting to think that following the cat's plan was a terrible idea. He stripped down until he was naked and then hopped into the freezing water of the lake. Puss stashed his clothes behind a large boulder so they were out of sight.

"Now throw yourself around in the water as if you're drowning," Puss said.

"But the water isn't even that deep—"

"Just do it!"

Against his better judgment, John threw himself about in the water as if he were in distress.

Soon, the king's carriage traveled down the road beside the lake. Puss ran out in front of it, waving his paws in the air, and got the driver to stop.

The king poked his head outside. "What's going on?" he asked.

"Thank heavens you're here, Your Majesty!" Puss said. "My master, the Marquis of Carabas, has been robbed! The assaulter stole his clothes, pushed him into the lake, and took off with his carriage! He'll drown if we don't rescue him."

The king was alarmed. "Guards, rescue the man in the lake immediately!" he ordered.

The king's guards threw John a rope and pulled him out of the water. By the time John was out of the lake, he was so cold that his body was blue and he was shivering madly. The guards wrapped him in their coats and let him sit in the carriage with the king and the princess where it was warm.

John couldn't believe he was in the presence of royalty. He was afraid Puss's plan would end horribly if he didn't know what he was doing.

"Are you all right, my boy?" the king said.

"Thanks to you, Your Majesty," John said. "I can't thank you enough for stopping to help me."

"What a horrible thing, to be robbed of one's clothes and pushed into a lake," the king said.

Unfortunately, the worst of winter was still to come. The snow fell more heavily and the air became even colder. Conditions became so bad that Thumbelina grew worried she wouldn't survive to see spring. She knocked on the door of the next home she found to ask for shelter. It was the underground home of a sweet little mouse.

"Can I help you?" the mouse asked.

"Please, I'm freezing and I have nowhere to go," Thumbelina said. "Might I come inside and get warm?"

"You poor dear," the mouse said. "Of course you can come inside."

The mouse had a kind soul and took Thumbelina in. She let her stay in her home through the harshest parts of the winter and the two became fast friends. Thumbelina earned her keep by helping the mouse keep her home clean. At night before bed, the mouse enjoyed listening to Thumbelina recite all the stories the widow had told her.

The mouse could tell that Thumbelina missed the widow greatly. But since it seemed unlikely she would ever find the widow, the mouse thought of another solution for her friend's loneliness.

The following night, the mouse invited the mole who lived next door to dinner. He was gruff and older and spoke of nothing but how much he hated sunlight. Even though Thumbelina disagreed entirely, she was very polite and listened to the mole.

The mole became quite taken with Thumbelina and she caught him

whispering into the mouse's ear whenever she wasn't looking. Later that evening, once Thumbelina and the mouse were alone, she found out what they were up to.

"The mole would like to marry you," the mouse said and smiled at the idea.

"That's very nice, but I can't marry a mole," Thumbelina said.

"Why not?" the mouse said. "He's just as lonely as you and lives in a large hole with plenty of rooms."

"But I'm not a mole," Thumbelina said.

"Then what exactly *are* you?" the mouse asked.

"I don't know what I am, but it's definitely not a creature that enjoys living in the dark ground," she said.

The mouse crossed her arms and glared at her. Although she didn't mean to, Thumbelina knew she had hurt the mouse's feelings. She had outworn her welcome, and it was time to leave.

By the time Thumbelina left the mouse's underground home, winter had ended and the first days of spring had arrived. All the birds had flown back from the south, and Thumbelina saw a familiar face circling above her.

"Thumbelina!" said the sparrow. "I've found it—I've found your home! I flew past it on my way back from the south!"

Thumbelina's heart began to race with happiness.

"I miss my mother so much," Thumbelina said. "Will you please take me there?"

"I would be happy to!" the sparrow said.

The bird landed beside her, and Thumbelina climbed on his back. He flew south for miles and miles. Thumbelina didn't realize she had traveled so far away from home.

"There it is!" the sparrow said. "Welcome home, Thumbelina."

The bird did not land at the widow's house as she had expected. Instead, he descended into an enchanted garden filled with thousands of beautiful flowers.

To Thumbelina's amazement, in the center of the garden was a tiny kingdom made of homes and buildings the size of birdhouses. It was

populated by men, women, and children her exact size. The only dif-
ference between them was that everyone in the kingdom had wings.

"What is this place?" Thumbelina asked.

"You mean you've never been here before?" the sparrow asked. "As
soon as I saw it, I was certain it was where you're from."

It was the first time she had ever seen people like her. Learning she
was not alone was a dazzling discovery. Just then, a little man came to
greet Thumbelina and the sparrow. He was very handsome and wore a
crown made of daisy petals.

"Hello," he said. "May I help you?"

"Yes, can you tell me where we are?" Thumbelina asked.

"You're in the Fairy Kingdom," he said.

"So I must be a *fairy*," Thumbelina said.

"You mean you didn't know?" the man asked.

Thumbelina told him how she had been born in the widow's house
and lived there until she was kidnapped. The man was fascinated by her
adventures trying to return home. He turned out to be a fairy prince,
and he gave her a tour of the kingdom.

"But if I'm a fairy, then where are my wings?" she asked.

"Wings aren't given; they're earned," the prince said. "But after the
journey you've been through, I think you deserve a pair."

The prince gave Thumbelina her very own pair of wings. They

magically attached to her back, and the prince taught her how to fly. Over time, the two fell in love and the prince asked Thumbelina to marry him.

The two were married in the garden, and Thumbelina was crowned a fairy princess. Even though she was among her own people, the fairy kingdom didn't feel like home without her mother. So Thumbelina and the prince found the widow and invited her to live with the fairies. The widow moved to the gardens to be closer to her daughter, and neither she nor Thumbelina was ever lonesome again.

The End

THE GINGERBREAD MAN

ADAPTED FROM THE
TRADITIONAL STORY

Once upon a time, there was a talented baker who lived in a small village. He and his wife had their own bakery, which was famous for having the best baked goods in town. Every morning, the villagers would line up outside to purchase his bread, muffins, and sweet rolls when they were fresh from the oven.

Even though he never received a complaint about his selection, the baker thought it was time to give his customers a little variety. He found a recipe to make gingerbread cookies and purchased the needed ingredients. He brought them back to his bakery and mixed them into dough.

The baker cut the dough into the shapes of little men and spread them over a cooking tray. Using frosting, he painted eyes, mouths, vests, buttons, pants, and little shoes on the cookies and put the tray into the oven. Soon the entire town was filled with the sweet scent of freshly baked gingerbread. Before he knew it, there was a line of hungry villagers outside the bakery's door.

What the baker didn't know at the time was that he had accidentally purchased flour that had a pinch of magic in it. So when the cookies were finished baking, he opened the oven—and one Gingerbread Man leaped off the tray and ran around the bakery.

"Run, run as fast as you can! You can't catch me. I'm the Gingerbread Man!" the cookie sang.

The baker made a mess in his bakery trying to seize the enchanted cookie, but it was too fast to catch. The Gingerbread Man ran out the door and through the village, laughing hysterically as he went.

"Run, run as fast as you can! You can't catch me. I'm the Gingerbread Man!" he sang to taunt the villagers.

The cookie looked delicious, so all the villagers chased after the Gingerbread Man, with the baker leading the charge. The Gingerbread Man was faster than all of them.

He ran through the countryside and passed by several mills and farms. The farm animals smelled him coming a mile away and stared at the cookie with hungry eyes.

"Run, run as fast as you can! You can't catch me. I'm the Gingerbread Man!" he sang to tease the animals.

The farm animals jumped over their fences and climbed out of their pens and ran after the Gingerbread Man too. They joined the villagers and the baker and created a massive stampede. The cookie

still ran much faster than them, and he giggled with joy.

The Gingerbread Man ran by a castle and caught the attention of the king and all the king's men.

"Run, run as fast as you can! You can't catch me. I'm the Gingerbread Man!" he sang to torment the king.

The king was insulted by the Gingerbread Man's taunting song and ordered his soldiers to capture the defiant cookie. The soldiers climbed aboard their horses and joined the stampede of animals and villagers. But alas, the Gingerbread Man was still much faster, and it didn't seem likely he would ever be caught.

Soon, the Gingerbread Man's journey came to a pause at the edge of a river flowing through the kingdom. Being made of flour, he knew he would disintegrate if he swam across.

"Oh no! What shall I do now?" he said.

"Don't worry, little cookie," said a fox who appeared beside him. "I know what it's like to be hunted and chased. I'll swim across the river, and you can ride on my back!"

The Gingerbread Man was delighted by the assistance. He climbed on top of the fox's back just as all the king's soldiers, the farm animals, the villagers, and the baker reached the river. They knew they would never catch him now.

The Gingerbread Man sang and danced when he saw all their long faces.

"Run, run as fast as you can! You can't catch me. I'm the—"

Before he could finish his song, the fox gobbled up the Gingerbread Man.

"My compliments to the baker!" the fox said and licked his lips.

The king's soldiers returned to the castle, the farm animals returned to the farm, the villagers returned to the village, the baker returned to the bakery, and they all returned to their normal lives.

The baker learned a very valuable business lesson: Always double-check your ingredients when trying new endeavors. If you add legs to something, it might just get up and run away.

The End

THE UGLY DUCKLING

ADAPTED FROM
HANS CHRISTIAN ANDERSEN

MOTHER GOOSE'S
NURSERY RHYMES

LITTLE BO PEEP

Little Bo Peep has lost her sheep,
And doesn't know where to find them;
Leave them alone, and they'll come home,
Wagging their tails behind them.

LITTLE MISS MUFFET

Little Miss Muffet

Sat on a tuffet,

Eating her curds and whey;

Along came a spider

Who sat down beside her

And frightened Miss Muffet away.

JACK AND JILL

Jack and Jill went up the hill,

To fetch a pail of water;

Jack fell down, and broke his crown,

And Jill came tumbling after.

When up Jack got and off did trot,

As fast as he could caper,

To old Dame Dob, who patched his nob

With vinegar and brown paper.

JACK BE NIMBLE

Jack be nimble, Jack be quick,
Jack jump over the candle-stick.

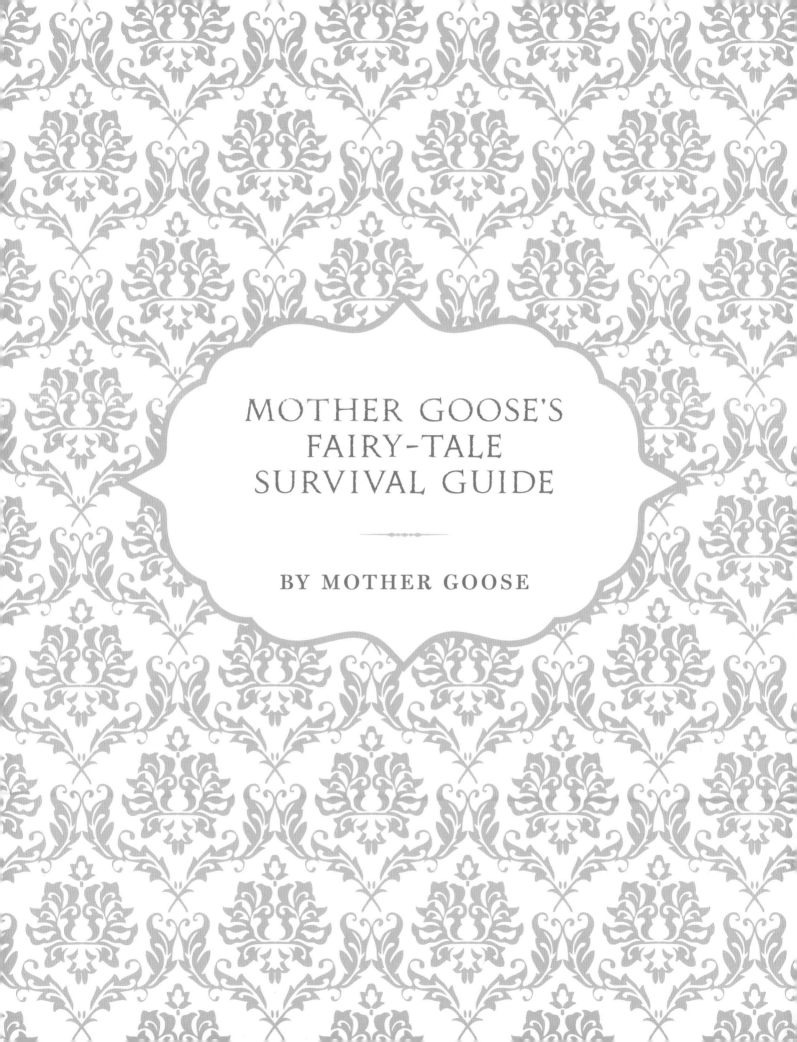

MOTHER GOOSE'S FAIRY-TALE SURVIVAL GUIDE

———

BY MOTHER GOOSE

Have you noticed anything funny about your *Treasury*? Have the pages started glowing at random times and become brighter every day? Is this glowing followed by a strange but inviting humming noise? Did you lean too far into the book and wind up falling into a different dimension? Then you're in luck, because this survival guide is for you!

When you purchased this book from the store, or checked it out from the library, or "borrowed" it from a friend, you probably weren't expecting it to transport you into a world where fairy tales are real. Life is full of surprises; sometimes it rains when it's supposed to be sunny, and sometimes children's books turn out to be portals into different dimensions. Relax; these things happen.

So if you find yourself in a fairy tale, there's no reason to panic. The fairy-tale world can be a very dangerous place, but if you follow my instructions carefully, you'll be back in your own world before you can say "and they all lived happily ever after." (Trust me, if there's one thing I'm good at, it's *surviving*. You're in good hands.)